First Novels

Think Again, Robyn

Hazel Hutchins
Illustrated by Yvonne Cathcart

Formac Publishing Company Limited
Halifax, Nova Scotia

Formac Publishing Company Limited acknowledges the financial support of
the Government of Canada through the Canada Book Fund for our publishing
activities. We acknowledge the support of the Canada Council for the Arts
which last year invested $24.3 million in writing and publishing throughout
Canada.

Canadä

Library and Archives Canada Cataloguing in Publication

Hutchins, H. J. (Hazel J.)
        Think again, Robyn / Hazel Hutchins ; illustrated by Yvonne
Cathcart.

(First novels)
Issued also in electronic format.
ISBN 978-1-4595-0078-5 (bound).--ISBN 978-1-4595-0077-8 (pbk.)

        I. Cathcart, Yvonne II. Title. III. Series: First novels.

PS8565.U826T29 2012   jC813'.54   C2012-902329-9

Formac Publishing Company Limited   Distributed in the United States by:
5502 Atlantic Street   Orca Book Publishers
Halifax, Nova Scotia,   P.O. Box 468
Canada B3H 1G4   Custer, WA U.S.A.
www.formac.ca   98240-0468

Printed and bound in Canada
Manufactured by Friesens Corporation in Altona, Manitoba, Canada in
August 2012.
Job #77084

Table of Contents

1

Name Game

Sometimes Grant Smith really makes me mad.

"Tony the Phony," he said as he walked by Tony at the recess doors.

"Robyn the Goblin," he laughed as he passed Marie and me on the stairs.

"Shelly the Smelly," he called as he raced past Shelly at the big rock.

It was the last one that got to me. Tony can take care of himself and I don't care what Grant the Ant calls me. But Shelly is different.

Shelly doesn't have a lot of friends. I can't explain why. She isn't mean. She doesn't bother anyone. Mostly she just sits by herself on the big rock at the end of the pavement. It makes me really mad if anyone teases Shelly. Especially Grant.

Grant Smith can find a zillion ways to bug people without even trying. And if you let him see that you're mad, things just get worse. I know all about Grant Smith. I've had experience.

As he raced away across the playing field, I went and sat by Shelly.

"Just ignore Grant," I said.

"Yup," said Shelly.

"You sit here a lot, don't you," I said.

"Mostly," she said.

"Is there a reason?" I asked.

"Nope," she said.

It's hard to talk to Shelly. She's quiet. I run out of things to talk about — really fast.

"Do you want to play hopping tag with Marie and me?" I asked.

"No thanks," said Shelly.

"Do you want to hang on the monkey bars?" I asked.

"Nope," said Shelly. "I like to just sit and look."

I'm not good at sitting — but I felt like it would be really mean to get up and walk away. That's when I had a great idea.

"Do you want to come over to my place tomorrow morning?" I asked.

Marie usually hangs out at my place on Saturday mornings. But this Saturday she and her brothers were heading to the local TV station. They were going to try and win tickets to a big hockey game next Thursday. Marie and her family really, really like hockey.

I'm not a fan. I don't play hockey so I don't know the rules and I don't get excited about it either. I'd be hanging out at my place Saturday morning. And if I asked Shelly over, I wouldn't feel guilty about leaving her alone on the rock. Shelly was already smiling.

"That would be great, Robyn," she said. "I'll bring my dolls."

Dolls? Oh no!

My heart sank down to my toes. I used to play with dolls when I was little ... sort of. And I know some kids still play with them and that's okay. But I outgrew dolls long ago. How could I tell Shelly that?

I put a big smile on my face.

"Super!" I said. "Talk to you later!"

I raced across the playground, tagged Marie and started hopping like crazy. When you've only got so much time, you have to pile in as much action as you can.

2

Team Cheer

Marie and I walked home together after school. She was getting really excited about tomorrow.

"Yo. Yo. Go Team Go!"

That was the cheer she'd made up for the TV station. Now she began doing weird dance moves all down the sidewalk.

"Do people always get this excited

about a hockey game?" I asked.

"Robyn, it's the finals!" said Marie. "The tickets sold out weeks ago. The station has the only tickets left. Every hockey fan in the world *really* wants those tickets!"

"Hockey fans like Grant?" I asked.

"Especially Grant. Grant is totally hockey-crazy," said Marie.

"I hope you win the tickets," I said.

"So do I," said Marie.

"And *don't* give them to Grant," I said.

"I won't," said Marie. Marie knows Grant and I don't get along. Marie doesn't get along with him either.

"Make sure you watch, okay?" she said. "Eleven-thirty tomorrow morning. Channel 7."

"I'll get Shelly to watch too," I said. "She's coming over to my place."

Marie stopped dancing. She bit her lip and looked like she wasn't sure if she should say something or not.

"It's okay," I said. "Shelly already told me she's bringing her dolls."

Marie giggled.

"Sorry, but I know how much you hate dolls." she said. And then she added without giggling "But Shelly *is* a nice girl, Robyn. I'm glad you invited her over."

Marie's mind flipped back to hockey, hockey, hockey. Red is her favourite hockey team's colour and she and her brothers had big plans.

"We're going to dress in red, and spray our hair and paint our faces to match," she said. "And there's a second part to the cheer."

She began to do the dance moves backwards this time.

"Go Team Go! Yo. Yo. Yo."

3

Shelly's Way

Shelly arrived at my apartment on Saturday morning, right on time. She was carrying a suitcase.

I was ready for her. I took her down to my bedroom. I'd set out all kinds of things to do — things that weren't dolls. I had my best games, my fancy art paper, my modelling clay that isn't even the fake kind and lots of other things. Shelly ignored them all.

She set the suitcase on the bed and opened it. *Poof.* Out sprang a gazillion tiny clothes and four fashion dolls. This was going to be even worse than I'd thought.

Shelly was so happy, however, that I tried to look interested.

"These are for you in case you don't have your own," she said, handing me two of the dolls.

Two dolls? I didn't even want one!

"Thanks," I said. "I don't need them both."

I gave one of the dolls back to her. She looked even happier.

She dressed all three dolls in evening

clothes and set them by my curtains. They looked like they were singers on a stage.

She dressed the dolls in bathing suits and set them by my blue and white pillows. They looked like they were at the ocean.

She dressed them in yellow, orange and green. She set them on the window ledge. With the sun streaming in they made me think of spring.

Weird. Every time she did something it came out looking like a picture.

It took me a long time to decide how to dress my doll. Shelly had used lots of bright colours and I wasn't feeling in that kind of mood. Suddenly I had an idea.

I dressed my doll in black. I set her by my wooden jewelry box. I put some tiny,

plastic flowers beside her.

"It's a funeral," I said. Shelly's expression changed completely. Oh no — maybe someone in her family had just died. I was trying to be nice but maybe I was being horrible without even meaning to!

The only thing bothering Shelly, however, was the silver buckles on the doll's shoes.

"Plain black would be better," she said. She switched them.

After that, no matter what else I tried to get Shelly to do, all she wanted was to play dolls. By the time she went home I was in a doll-induced stupor. Even when the phone rang, I didn't remember that I'd forgotten something important.

4

A Big Win

"Did you see us? Were we great? The TV station was really, really fun!"

Marie's voice on the phone was super excited.

"Oh no — I forgot to watch!" I said.

"Robyn!" exclaimed Marie.

"I'm sorry Marie," I said. "I really am."

"Good thing my mom recorded it,"

said Marie. "You can watch next time you're over. It really was exciting!"

"You mean you won the tickets?" I asked.

"No," said Marie. "Didn't Shelly tell you?"

"Tell me what?" I asked.

"Her dad won the tickets!" said Marie. "He works right by the station. He heard about the contest, walked across the street and entered. He's taking Shelly to the big game. He said so right on television!"

Shelly's dad? That was great! I might not know a lot about hockey but I do know that if you ever want to be popular at our school, just win tickets to a big game. Shelly wouldn't be sitting alone any more. And I wouldn't have to be the one sitting with her!

When we arrived at school on Monday morning, everything was exactly the way I thought it would be. Lots of kids had been at the station so everyone knew about the tickets without Shelly even telling them. Without saying a word, she'd gone from "the kid who always sits alone" to "the kid everyone is talking to."

"Are they good seats?" asked Ari.

"Were you really excited when your dad told you?" asked Marie.

"Who's your favourite player?" asked Linden.

"Corval is the best ever!" said Grant. "Get me his autograph! Please?"

Grant definitely wasn't calling Shelly rhyming names any more.

Shelly looked like she wasn't quite

sure what to say. That's how it is when you aren't used to a lot of attention. But I knew she'd get the hang of it.

"Shelly doesn't need me anymore," I told Marie. "Let's go play."

"Maybe later," said Marie. "Being around Shelly is exciting."

The excitement spilled over into the classroom. Even our teacher got involved.

"Shelly, instead of handing in a piece of journal writing for Language Arts class this Friday, would you like to do a presentation instead?" asked Mr. Wagner. "You can be a reporter. You can describe what the big game was like."

Once again, Shelly looked like she didn't know what to say. I nodded across the room to encourage her.

"I could try," she said at last.

"Make it about Corval scoring the winning goal," shouted Grant. "Yes!"

"Can our class have fun too?" asked Marie. "Can we have a party with team colours and cheers and music and food? We could do it Thursday before the game."

Mr. Warner agreed. Everyone likes a party. Now Shelly was a hero even with the kids who weren't hockey fans. Things were getting better and better.

But on the way home from school something strange happened. Marie was busy after class so I was walking home alone. I thought I heard footsteps behind me. I spun around. The person behind me jumped about a foot.

"Shelly?" I asked.

"I've got a problem, Robyn," said Shelly. "Do you know anything about hockey?"

5

Quackers

"If you ever decide to be nice to someone, make sure the hockey finals aren't going on."

That's what I told the Kelly twins Monday night. The twins are named Abigail and Angie and they live in the apartment next door. I was playing with them so Mr. Kelly could get some paperwork done.

"Moo," said Abigail and handed me a zebra.

"Oink," said Angie and handed me a hippo.

Not quite right ... but close enough when you're only two years old.

"And another thing," I said to the twins. "Make sure the person you're *trying* to be nice to doesn't have a dad who wins tickets to the big game."

Mr. Kelly looked up from his paperwork.

"Who won the tickets, Robyn?" he asked.

"Shelly's dad," I said. "Except he found out he has to go out of town. And Shelly's not a big enough hockey fan to want to go to the game without him. They gave the tickets away."

Mr. Kelly shook his head.

"That's too bad," he said.

"It gets worse," I told him. "When Shelly got to school on Monday, all the kids thought she still had tickets and they were so excited that Shelly didn't know how to tell them she *wasn't* going. So now she's pretending she *is* going and she even has to do a report on the game for school."

"I'm confused," said Mr. Kelly. "She has to do a report on the game she isn't going to?"

"Right," I said. "But don't worry. I'm going to help her with the report — from watching TV."

One of the things I like about Mr. Kelly is that he doesn't nag me about what's right or what's wrong, at least not for something like this. I already knew this wasn't exactly honest but I didn't think it was hurting anyone either. It wasn't exactly a lie. It was just a bit of a cover-up. Mr. Kelly did have something else to say though.

"TV might not be enough, Robyn," he said. "I think a lot of things happen in the arena that people don't see on TV. But I can't help you because I've never been to one of the games."

"Quack, quack, quack, quack!" shouted the twins.

They were each holding up a giraffe.

Yup, that was just about the way my life was going at the moment.

6

Hurrah for Marie's Brothers

That night I asked my mom a question.

"How come you've never taken me to a hockey game? I mean the kind with famous players and a bunch of screaming fans?"

"Robyn," said my mom. "You don't like hockey. I don't like hockey. The tickets cost a lot of money."

Good answer. But I had another question.

"Do you know *anyone* who has ever been to that kind of game?"

"I think one of Marie's brothers went to a pre-season game last year," said Mom. "Would that count?"

Marie's family — of course! And I even had an excuse to go over to Marie's house because I still hadn't seen her on TV.

The next day when I asked Marie if I could come to her place after school, she didn't suspect a thing. Two of her older brothers were home too. Once we were watching the recording of Marie's family at the rally on TV, it was easy to get her brothers talking. Both had been to professional hockey games.

"Did you really want to win the tickets?' I asked. "I mean, you have a big TV. What's different if you go to a game? Don't you already see it all on TV anyway?"

"Not if you're down by the ice," said brother number one. "If you have seats near the ice you really notice how fast the players skate. And the sound when they hit the boards — whoa! Impressive."

"Neat," I said. "Is there other stuff?"

"There's the excitement," said brother number two. "Actually being in the crowd is different than watching from home. And there's the jumbotron, the huge score board above centre ice. It does a super job on the replays. Even the ads are great on the jumbotron."

"They are?" I asked. I began to make notes on the pad of paper by the phone. "Anything else?"

"Little kids like the mascot," said brother number one. "He makes fun of the other team all through the game."

"And people throw T-shirts and water bottles into the crowd to get everyone to cheer louder," said brother number two. "You don't get to go home with free stuff when you watch the game on TV."

They practically wrote the report for me! As she walked me back to my place, however, Marie kind of burst my bubble.

"Shelly's not really going to the game, is she?" asked Marie.

So much for trying to fool my best friend. Marie listened carefully as I

explained how things had gone wrong.

"Are you going to tell?" I asked.

"Shelly has enough trouble making friends as it is. I won't tell," said Marie. "But both of you better *really* watch the game on TV because I won't cover for you. You may be okay with telling lies, but I'm not."

Thanks Marie. Sort of.

7

Go, go, go!

The party on Thursday afternoon was a big success. Our class played hockey bingo and ate lots of cupcakes with red icing. After class, Shelly went home to get her suitcase. Then she came over to my place. We sat in front of the TV. I had my notebook. Shelly had the dolls.

There were six of them this time. They

were all dressed in red. Shelly arranged them on boxes and cushions in front of the TV. It was like a picture again — fans watching a game. She even posed their plastic bodies to make things look exciting.

And the hockey game *was* exciting, right from the start.

"Go! Go, go, go!"

That was me yelling at the TV. Corval had the puck and was skating like crazy down the ice.

Suddenly the other team stole the puck. Three players swooped towards our goal.

"No!"

Then suddenly — yes! Corval had the puck again.

"Go! Go, go, go!"

Back and forth. Back and forth. Right

up to the first break for commercials. Whew! I needed a break too.

"Let's rearrange the dolls," said Shelly.

Arghh. All of a sudden, it was just too much. I took a deep breath. My teeth were gritted but I tried not to sound mad.

"Shelly," I said. "I don't like dolls."

Her face fell. I hurried to add the rest of it — because there *was* more.

"But *you* can still play them," I said. "It's fine by me. It's neat the way you always make it look like a scene in a play or a movie. Maybe you'll be something interesting like a movie director when you grow up."

Right away Shelly was back to smiling again.

"Actually, I want to be a fashion

designer," said Shelly. "I didn't have enough red clothes for today so I made some of the scarves and hats. Can you tell?"

I picked up one of the dolls and looked closely. I could tell — but only in a good way. It was amazing. A lot of kids say they want to be something neat when they grow up but Shelly was already teaching herself. And suddenly I understood the way she kept posing the dolls.

"You set them up like it's a fashion show," I said. "Or a display in a store window. Or a photographer taking pictures for a fashion magazine!"

Shelly looked thoughtfully at the dolls.

"I didn't think about the photographer part," she said. "Maybe I could borrow Dad's camera and try taking pictures. I'd have a

record of what I've done. Great idea Robyn!"

The crowd roared, which meant the ads were over and the game had started again. I turned back to the TV. Yup, Corval had the puck.

"Go. Go. Go!"

8

Just Plain Grumpy

When the home team loses an important game, there are more heart attacks, more fights and more all-around grumpy people for a full three days afterwards. Mr. Kelly says it's a fact he found on the Internet.

It's also true in real life. Our team lost the game that Thursday. I was really grumpy the next day. Shelly was grumpy

too. And the kids at school who are big hockey fans were super, triple grumpy.

"We should have changed goalies way sooner," complained Marie the next morning.

"The reffing didn't go our way once. It was like they were all blind," said Ari.

"Don't even talk to me about Corval!" wailed Grant.

After that, no one wanted to talk about it. Not during attendance. Not during Math. When Language Arts rolled around and it was time for Shelly to give her report, Grant called out in the loudest voice ever.

"Nooo! Don't make me suffer all over again!"

"Grant, you are being rude," said Mr. Warner. "Shelly, go ahead, please."

Shelly stood up with her report in her hand. We'd written it together. It had the speed of the players and the "wham" of the boards. It had the jumbotron, the mascot and water bottles flying through the air to the crowd. It had descriptions of people in the stands that Shelly had taken from the crowd shots on TV. It had the excitement of the goals. It had the disappointment of the ending.

But Shelly didn't read the report. She just stood there. The silence got longer and longer. Finally she took a deep breath.

"I think I'd rather just tell the truth," she said. "I didn't actually go to the game."

Before I could worry about what would happen next, Grant took over.

"THANK GOODNESS!" he called

from the back of the class.

Even Mr. Warner was relieved.

"Maybe it's for the best after all," he said. "It was a pretty painful game."

"Could I just do a regular journal entry and hand it in next week instead?" asked Shelly.

Mr. Warner nodded.

And just as easy as that, the cover-up was over.

9

Robyn's Victory

When recess arrived that morning, Marie and I raced around the playground three times, really fast, non-stop. Then we went and sat by Shelly.

"It was a good report. It would have worked," I said.

"I know," said Shelly. "But I got tired of pretending I had tickets when I didn't.

Kind of like you got tired of pretending about dolls."

"You were really brave to tell the truth in front of the whole class," said Marie.

"Are you mad Robyn?" asked Shelly.

I almost said no. But then I remembered my new policy. I wasn't going to pretend around Shelly any more.

"I'm a little bit mad," I admitted. "I'm mad at *myself* for not just helping you tell everyone the truth in the first place."

Then I frowned really hard.

"And I'm *really* mad at the hockey game because I wasted an entire evening watching it."

Marie and Shelly both laughed.

"Hah!" said Marie. "Shelly already told me you were yelling at the TV set just like my

brothers do. You're probably going to end up being a bigger hockey fan than Grant."

I smiled. I *had* been excited about the game. I was even thinking I'd like to watch a game with Marie's family or Mr. Kelly so I could learn the rules and understand it better.

But before I could tell Marie, the school doors burst open. Grant had stayed late to finish some work and now he was heading out onto the playing field.

"Marie the Flea," he called as the doors thumped against the door stops.

"Robyn the Goblin," he called as he took the stairs three at a time.

"Shelly the …"

That's when something unexpected happened. I didn't get mad at Grant. That was good. Getting mad just gives Grant more reasons to tease. But I didn't just sit there either.

"Cut it out, Grant," I called. The matter-of-fact tone of my voice surprised even me. "No one cares."

It was true. Or at least it was partly true. Name calling isn't ever good but somehow — in this case at least — it seemed to have lost its power. I don't know if Shelly will ever have a lot of friends but she definitely has Marie and me on her side.

Grant shrugged. I'd won! Now that he wasn't getting a rise out of us, he didn't care much either.

But I couldn't help it. I had to add one more thing.

"And if you don't stop calling names

we'll take turns describing — over and over — how Corval missed the final big shot in double overtime," I said.

Grant pressed his hands against his ears.

"Ahhhhhhh!" he shouted.

And he raced away as fast as he could.

More novels in the First Novels series!

Robyn's Monster Play

Hazel Hutchins

Illustrated by Yvonne Cathcart

Robyn starts her own play, The Monster that Ate the World, and learns how difficult it is to organize everything by herself.

Morgan and the Dune Racer

Ted Staunton

Illustrated by Bill Slavin

It's Morgan's birthday and all he wants is Charlie's remote-control toy no matter what it takes or who he hurts to get it.

Lilly Traps the Bullies
Brenda Bellingham
Illustrated by Clarke
MacDonald

Lilly has to make a decision: choose between old friends and the gang of cool kids.

Mia, Matt and the Lazy Gator
Annie Langlois
Illustrated by Jimmy Beaulieu
Translated by Sarah Cummins

Mia and Matt can't wait to get to their uncle's summer cottage and find out what animal will be the star of their vacation. Will they be able to teach a lazy gator to dance?

Music by Morgan

Ted Staunton

Illustrated by Bill Slavin

Morgan has to get creative, and sneaky, if he wants to play music instead of floor hockey. He crafts a plan to swap places with Aldeen — but how long will they pull it off before they get caught?

Daredevil Morgan

Ted Staunton

Illustrated by Bill Slavin

Will Morgan be brave enough to try the GraviTwirl ride at the Fall Fair? Can he win the "Best Pumpkin Pie" contest, or will Aldeen Hummel, the Godzilla of grade three, interfere?

Raffi's For the Birds
Sylvain Meunier
Illustrated by Élisabeth Eudes-Pascal
Translated by Sarah Cummins

Raffi wants to save the birds by protesting the destruction of the trees they nest in. While he may have trouble walking, he has lots of ideas, and friends ready to help!